D0587313

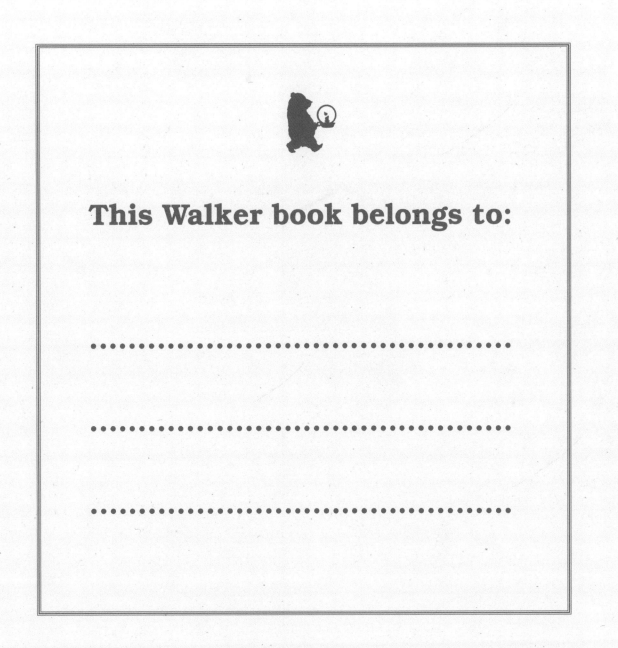

This Walker book belongs to:

....

....

....

To the small ones
~ J.B.

WALKER BOOKS
AND SUBSIDIARIES
LONDON · BOSTON · SYDNEY · AUCKLAND

First published 2009 by Walker Books Ltd
87 Vauxhall Walk, London SE11 5HJ

This edition published 2010

10 9 8 7 6 5 4 3 2 1

© 2009 John Burningham

The right of John Burningham to be identified as
author/illustrator of this work has been asserted
by him in accordance with the Copyright, Designs
and Patents Act 1988

This book has been typeset in ITC Bookman.

Printed in China

All rights reserved. No part of this book may be reproduced,
transmitted or stored in an information retrieval system in
any form or by any means, graphic, electronic or mechanical,
including photocopying, taping and recording, without prior
written permission from the publisher.

British Library Cataloguing in Publication Data: a catalogue
record for this book is available from the British Library

ISBN 978-1-4063-2611-6

www.walker.co.uk

IT'S A SECRET!

JOHN BURNINGHAM

In Marie Elaine's house

they had a cat whose name was Malcolm.
Every night Malcolm went out and
every morning he came back in.
During the day Malcolm slept a lot of the time.

"Where do cats go at night?" Marie Elaine asked.
"I don't know," said Marie Elaine's mother.
"They just go outside somewhere."

One evening in the summer,
Marie Elaine came down into the kitchen
to get a cold drink from the fridge.

There, by the cat flap, was Malcolm the cat,
and he was all dressed up in fancy clothes
and a hat.

"Why are you all dressed up like that and where are you going?" asked Marie Elaine.

"I'm going to a party," said Malcolm, "but I can't say where because it's a secret."

"Oh, please, please let me come with you. I'll keep your secret. Please, please let me come," said Marie Elaine.

Malcolm thought for a moment and then said, "All right, but you can't come like that, you'll have to put on something that's right for a party."

Marie Elaine raced up to her room and put on her party dress.

"That's all right, I suppose," said Malcolm, "but you'll have to get small."

Marie Elaine got small and they went out of the house through the cat flap.

Now, little Norman Kowalski was not asleep.
He was looking out of the window and saw
Marie Elaine and Malcolm.

 "I've seen you," said Norman. "Where are
you going and why are you small?"

"We're going to a party and, anyway, it's a secret," said Marie Elaine.

"Let me come," said Norman, "or I'll tell."

"Oh, all right then," said Malcolm, "but you must hurry. The party is starting soon and we have to get past the dogs."

They rounded a corner and suddenly
the dogs started to chase them.
They ran as fast as they could and
just managed to get to a fire escape.
They rushed up the stairs, and although
the dogs came after them ...

Malcolm knew a way where the dogs wouldn't follow.

Finally they arrived at the place
on top of the roofs where the party
was about to start.

There were lots and lots of cats, and some had come from a long way away.

The cats were very friendly to Marie Elaine and Norman

and danced with them and let them join in their party games.

Suddenly all the cats became quiet.
All you could hear was them whispering,
"She's coming. She's coming."

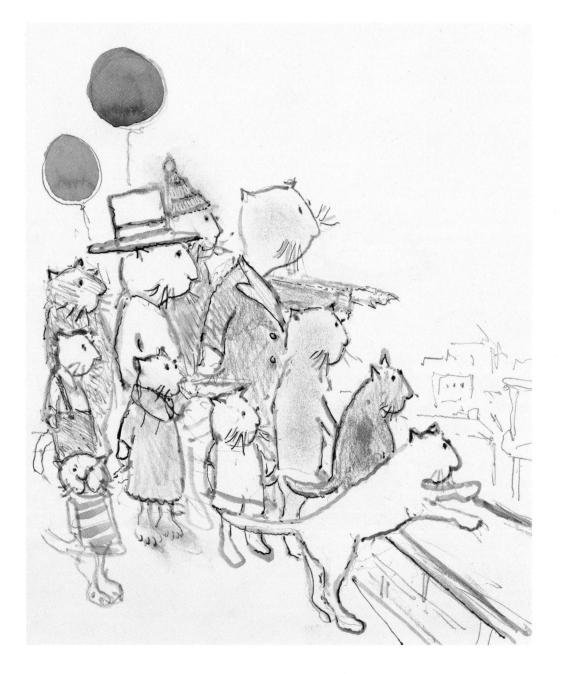

It was the Queen of the Cats.

They had a delicious midnight feast.

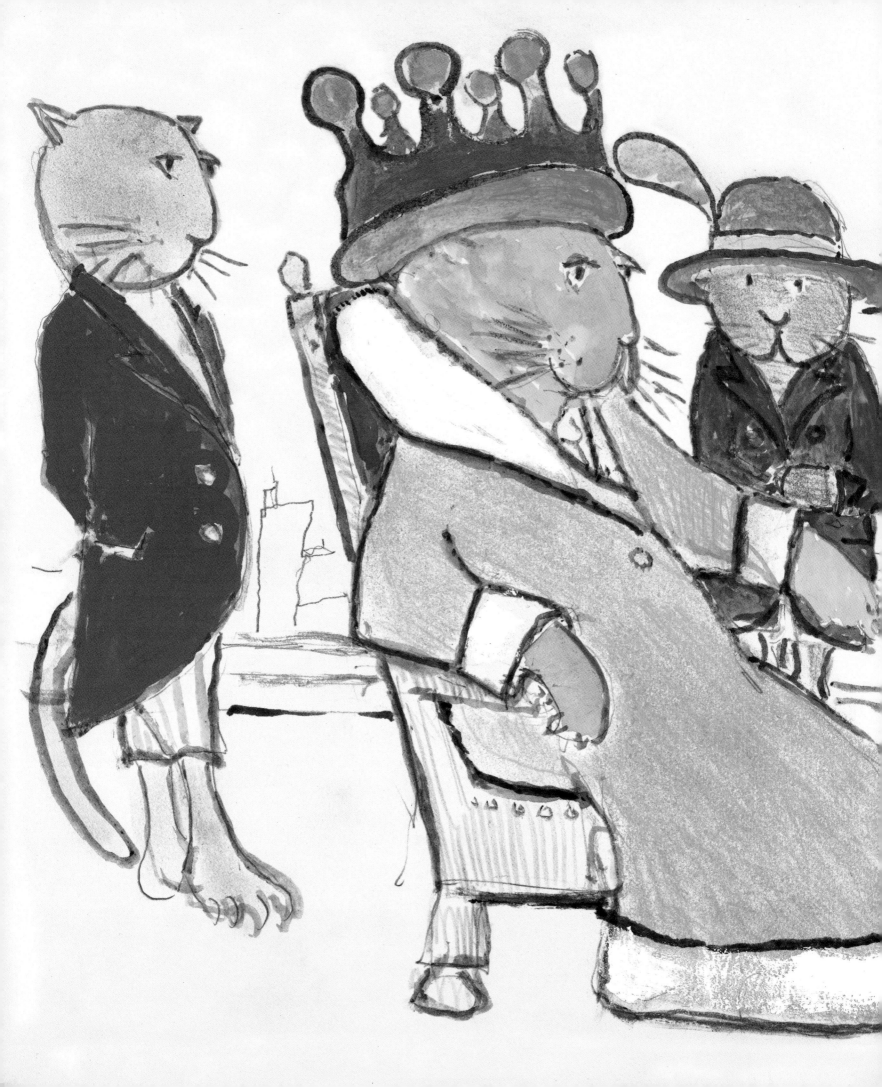

After the feast, the Queen gave
everyone presents to take home.
Marie Elaine was given a little doll,
which was a kitten, and Norman
was given a toy mouse.

Suddenly the Queen said, "Look at the time.
The party must end, it will be light soon."

Nobody wanted the party to end and none
of them wanted to leave and go home.

The cats all waved goodbye
and set off in different directions.

Malcolm showed Marie Elaine and Norman
the way back home over the rooftops.

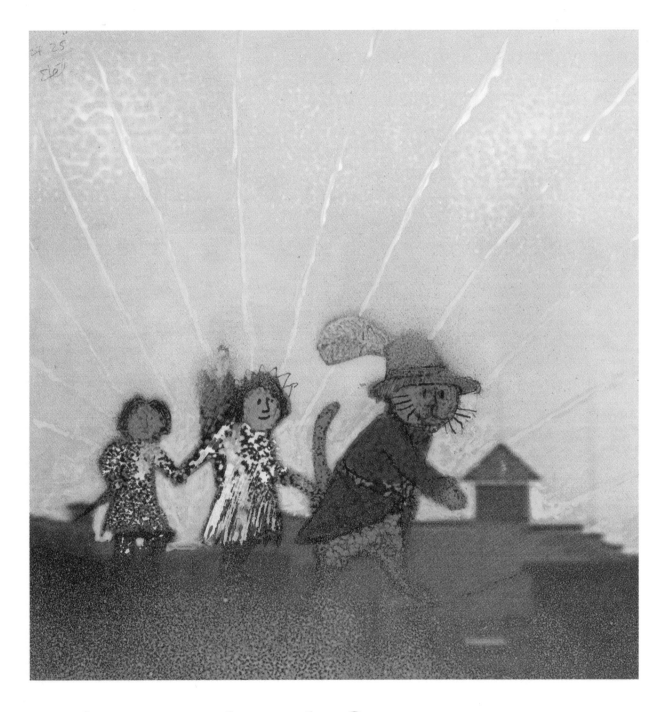

"When we go down the fire escape,
we must be very quiet because of the dogs,"
Malcolm said.

They went very quietly past the dogs,
who were asleep.

Then they hurried home as fast
as they could go.

When Marie Elaine got back to her house,
she was very tired and fell asleep on the sofa.

In the morning her mother was
surprised to see her downstairs.
"You look as if you were out
all night with the cat," she said.
"I was," said Marie Elaine, "and
I know where he goes at night.
But I can't tell you because
it's a secret."

Also by John Burningham

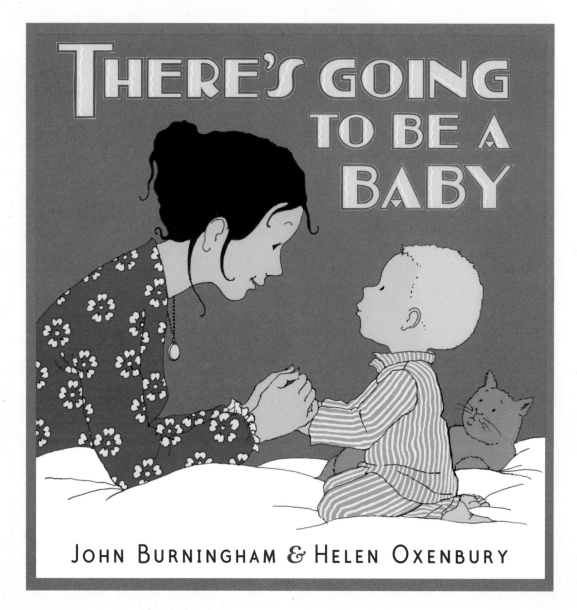

ISBN 978-0-7445-4996-6

Available from all good bookstores

www.walker.co.uk